FROM THE EYES OF A COSMONAUT

RUCHI SINGH

To my mom, dad and Srisht-thank you for making me the person I am

Contents

THE TYPEWRITER- death is the mother of poetry.

ONE

THE TYPEWRITER-DEATH IS THE MOTHER OF POETRY.

"The shadows, the impressions, the letters on wall,
The words, the leaves, the grass along the walk,
I call them up, come haunt me,
The sunlight, I keep it out,
It can burn me, I untrust it loud,
The moon, I feel is no more mine,
The stars won't listen, I don't want them to shine,
Shut them down, let them haunt me then,
The smell in the air reminds me of a peculiar time,
I feel the trees but I know they aren't alive,
Come wake them up, come haunt me then,
The rhymes I sing have a deadly voice,

The hand that could hold just shiver and die,
Well haunt me then, I don't know how to hide,
These feet can walk, they still walk over thorns,
These eyes still smile, they have nothing to feel,
The glory on my face would never tell the uneasy tale,
Come take a pen and pierce my head,
In the name of Satan, come haunt me then
The slate is blank, tell me the story to write,
The pages are bleached, my brain has gone blind,
The diaries I have are filled with blood,
Come haunt me then I want to let my fear cry."

"A very warm morning folks. The nightdream club, I remember I started this club when I was 19 years old, exactly 10 years ago. I remember everybody, including my parents, said I should basically concentrate on studies. Certainly, just existing and abiding by the rules of society is something they call a good living. In the whole process of being a good human, we certainly die a thousand times. Our dreams are somewhere buried deep in the soil. I wish there was a cemetery of dead dreams and right choices. I bet the entire land of this world, including the precious ocean beds, would never ever be able to provide shelter to their soul. Well, my heart goes out to all those dead dreams. One thing that I have learnt is that nothing comes for free. you should have the courage to fight, sometimes even against destiny. Most of times, destiny is a bitch. But if, if you're hard enough, if you choose to be a warrior even when you're bleeding with wounds that fate has given you, only and only then life gives you a chance to win over destiny. These people are rare, almost not in existence. But once in several eras, they're born to change a lot, to fight even when the battle ground seems so hollow, as if it will collapse.

But these warriors, they're stubborn for what they want. They fight in the air while their battle ground solidifies and once, they have this ground beneath their feet, they know it's time for triumph. Being successful is an extreme sport. Cherishing success is an art. Otherwise, many of us are born just to realise we are nothing but a body that obeys the unworthy rules of society. I also remember how difficult it was for me to be an engineer, more precisely, an engineering student from one of the most renowned colleges. For somebody, who has surrendered himself for meeting expectations of the family, coming out of the shell for opening a poetry club was really a difficult task, and that too at such a young age. Now I am here, standing in front of you. A successful engineer and luckily, owner of one the most successful poetry clubs in the city. Well, I am Zubair Hasan, for those who don't know me. It's been 10 years and we all have come a long way."

There were hundreds of people who congregated for the evening for rejoicing the tenth anniversary of the club. I always found the idea of being on stage abhorrent. Confidence and me were kind of rivals. But today I felt some different kind of confidence in me. I barely blinked on the stage. I was constantly staring at that one person, the sienna-coloured glitters of those brown eyes, occasionally being covered by flicks of hair, those cocoa-coloured hands coming over to put them back behind the ears that I suppose were listening to me. I must say, the girl was beautiful. Well, she wasn't the kind of beautiful that we often see in movies and daily soaps. I must say there's a lot of false idea regarding what true beauty is. She wasn't that perfect figure that could satisfy the testosteronic lust. She reflected poetries in her eyes. The curiosity that her expressions presented, was adorable as hell. In the whole room she was perhaps the only person who was able to sink deep into every word that I said. I used to notice her expressions when I used to stand on the dire. The wave of emotion on her face that came along with words that gushed out of my mouth, the matching of rhythm felt as if universe was trying to synchronise us together.

I didn't know even her name. But I knew that she had been a member of this club for long. She used to attend every meeting of the club. I have been noticing her for I don't know how many months and I could never really build the courage to talk to her. It would be a lie if I say that I wasn't I attracted towards her because not liking her felt like an illegitimate task, probably a punishable one.

"Anybody up for some good poem? "I inquired.

"Yes!" good gracious. She stood up and said "well, I have been a poetry lover and a member of this club for very long and finally I have somehow managed to assemble some meaningful words together" there was swarming nervousness in her words, expressions and actions. She was trying to dodge the crowd away, as if she was talking to herself. She wasn't really confident. But the cape of strength that she wore, that delusion, that pretence had something to admire.

"We would be blessed to know how beautifully those words are arranged." I said and she gave a smile. Anything I say to praise that smile won't be enough. The brilliance of that smile felt everlasting. I felt like I was standing somewhere in front of eternity. Is this what they call love? When you finally feel the existence of miracles, magic, heavenliness slowly spreading over hell, rage, fire, storm and blood. As it spreads, it covers the gloomy part, but not to forget the gloominess is never dead. It persists in the core.

She came up to stage and all this time I had been staring her. She, kind of blushed on making an eye contact with me. I gave her the mic and went down the stage. I sat on a seat in the front row. All this time, I made sure she was the only person I was looking at.
“Sometimes I wonder what life is,

Is it just a series of sarcasms, Sarcasms of time and universe?

Time pushes us towards risks that our souls fear the most, the universe pulls us away and shouts out to be aware,

Blood, skin, bones, power, immolation-oblation and necromancy, nothing could succeed in giving birth to a soul that hasn’t fallen into this trap,
We are all children of the universe and victim of time, we are all criminals who try to contradict reality whenever we show mercy to our own soul,
we call ourselves losers and winners, but we are just those innocent juvenile soul, filled with guilt and regrets, trying to destroy the existence of a part that resides in us which happens to be over kind and over merciful in a world that is filled with wrath of time and universe, who coined the word destiny, luck is nothing but a hallucination, what happens to you is nothing but a sarcasm of time and universe,

Who said God of mercy looks at you with pity, why do we always see happiness as an epitome of relief,

I wonder it’s pain that makes everything beautiful between

the jokes that the nature plays." She recited and gave a conscious smile. The whole room was filled with unison of applauds. Everything was just as musical as it could be.

Pain makes it beautiful. This phrase was like a weapon. It felt like it uncovered several holistic wounds on my soul and simultaneously it was creating a void for a new one. It was strange and comforting at the same time. That phrase was the only thing that was going through my mind for next few minutes. I stood up and all I kept glancing at her all this time.it was impossible to get my eyes off. She looked at me once or twice, but ignored me for most of the time.

After I came home, she was the only person I was thinking about. I was unable to sleep. I went to the typewriter. I started typing. But I couldn't concentrate. I wasn't able to write anything good or meaningful or I wrote but I wasn't satisfied. I opened my diary. I started reading the poems that I wrote a year or two years ago. They had pain. They were extraordinarily beautiful. I was expecting something like that to come out of me. The emptiness of my brain along with those blank pages that I was unable to fill, they were kind of irritating me. It seemed like emotional violence to be honest.

I don't know when did I fell asleep. The moment I opened my eyes, she was the only person I could see. It was all like a hallucination. It was like I was dying out of thirst and suddenly I saw a way out, I saw the source of nectar that has ability to keep me shielded away from all disastrous pain. I felt like I had been suffocating for a long time and finally, finally I learnt how to breathe. It was like I found a thin thread that was connecting my soul to life, but as I said the thread was really thin, fragile. I could feel that it can break any moment. It was risky but comforting.

The bell rang.

I opened the door. I saw her right in front of me. I was shocked. My expressions were similar to a person who would have seen a dead body in front of his house. I thrashed the door and closed it. I started hyperventilating. Sweat was dripping from my face. I took a tissue and wiped of the sweat off my face. I saw through the peephole. She was right there.

"Am I really terrifying?" she asked from outside.

I took out some tissues from the tissue roll beside the table. I cleaned by face and closed my eyes and helped myself to bring my breath back to normal. It took few minutes until I really felt oakayish. I finally managed to open the door.

"you know what? It has been 1 year 3 months and 18 days since I have joined the club. 56 meetings have been held since then. In every meeting, I have to face you. Every time when you give me that promising look, the only thing I could think of is that when will this stupid asshole build enough courage to come and ask me out. But today, I say the wait is over because I know that some assholes are always going to be an asshole and so you have to play the cupid for yourself. So, will you please spare some time from your job and the poetry club and can we please go out for... for a coffee?" she had been really confident all this time but her eyes stared at the ground when she said the last line. She blushed and that blush, my goodness, that was so intimate.

The redness of her cheeks was filling radiance in the ambience.

I could do nothing but fall for her a little more whenever I looked at her. I agreed to go out with her on a coffee date. We started meeting each other a little too often. She started coming to my place every once in a while. But I was still not sure if it was love or not. I wasn't sure if I was ready to admit and accept the fact that I had been in love all this while.

We decided to go for trekking on a mount nearby. It was a three-and-a-half-kilometre long trek. We decided to start early in the morning. We started at 5:30 A.M. we reached the top at about 8:00 A.M. It was a chill winter morning. Fogg was all around. The sky was filled with mist. The sun came out. But the rays could not reach us that clearly. Still a shining figure was visible through all the mist. She was hyperventilating, breathing as fast as she could. A thin, very thin layer of sweat occupied her face and that made her the glow on her face more stunning and perceptible. Every movement of her body was an exaggerated effort to kill exhaustion. All of it looked terribly beautiful. In that moment, it was honestly driving me crazy. I felt like holding her, slowly moving into her, to make love, for now and forever. I was so drowned inside my thoughts that I didn't notice I had been staring her for a long while now. She looked at me said,

"Do you know why are we all are so much in love with poetry?" She asked wiping the sweat off her face with a handkerchief.

Her question brought me back to reality. But I wasn't

completely into the reality and I found it hard to manage to think of a proper answer. I kept quiet and looked into her eyes. I felt like I had been trapped in something which was mysterious unusual but beautiful. I felt like I was slaved. I felt like there were cuffs around my wrist and I had nowhere to go. I want to be here forever. I don't know what forever is but this was my forever. I knew very well that forever like this push you into the necropolis. My will and my strength were compromised. I surrendered. I had no other choice. And I wondered, is this something we all call "love"?

"Because we all are humans. We unknowingly believe in keeping things uncompleted, leaving chapters unclosed, running away from what we love. Nothing but we ourselves are reason why we feel so tired at the end of the day. We are all busy in being strong and savage, we hardly realise that we have emotions too and that unknowingly we had been in love for too long now. And by the time we realise this fact, the bell rings and the time for heart break begins. We keep quiet not knowing what to say. Till the time we find the right words, we realise the heart that was supposed to listen, is no more there. In the whole process of hiding those feelings, we open up. We choose poetry where we close all the doors, but our human habits compel us to leave a loophole, expecting somebody may find that loophole, somebody may feel it and somebody may come.... For our rescue, to prevent us from almost dying. We find a heart to save us, we find a body that can make us feel warm, a mind that can feed life into a breathing corpse. But, as I said, we are all humans, we repeat the same cycle and we let everything go, just by being dishonest with our feelings." She continued. I could see her eyes gleaming with a little more tear. She was trying hard not to cry. But I could see, the brightness in her eyes, the strength in her voice was totally her darkness in disguise.

“Hmm.” I was thinking of a lot of things but all I could manage to say was this.

“Hmm. So, I choose not to repeat the same cycle again. I choose to be a rebellious human being this time. This time I choose to be a little more obstinate and I want to be honest and confess everything”. She looked down as if trying to hide a lot of emotions all at once.

“So, what do you want to confess?” I asked looking the other way.

“I love you and I don’t want you to be in my poems this time. I want you be in my life and our love in our poems” she said looking into my eyes. She was all calm. But her expressions were violent, depicting the energy of her emotions. The obstinacy in them showed her obsession, that this time it was do or die for her, that this time nothing can defeat her stubbornness, that this time it can go to any extent.

“Listen, I do have feelings for you. But I don’t know if it is as true and strong as yours. I need some time to think.” I spoke. My voice was firm. I wanted to be as clear as I could be.

“You can take your time.” She spoke.

We didn’t utter a single word on our way back. It was time to leave.

“The weather was beautiful in an unusual way today. It was never like this before. I feel like I have been living life for too long. And today it felt like forever.” She alleged.

I couldn’t manage to say anything. I went near her, and I took her hand into mine.

“I am sorry for making it hard for you” I Said.

“I will be waiting for an answer” she said and she left.

For next few days I was busy with my work. The company was really getting over my nerves. There were too many meetings scheduled and I overworked for almost a week. All this time she never tried to contact me.

I texted her a few times to know if she was fine. She used to say that she is fine and I don’t have to worry.

I sat on the typewriter to write something. I had too much inside me. But I couldn’t write anything. This thing was killing me bit by bit. I felt like there was no driving force inside me. The darkness around me was vanishing bit by bit and perhaps that was taking my words away.

I called Reyansh. Reyansh was my best friend since I was three. He probably knew me better than anyone else in the entire world. He was more than a soulmate. He could read into my silences and complete sentences that were difficult for me to complete. I told him everything and he listened patiently.

"I think you really love her. I know you have been through some bad times and I know how reluctant and cynical you are at this moment. Take your own time, man. You don't need to stress too much. You are going to figure it out soon." He said trying to comfort me. His words made me feel good for a very little while.

"Yeah" I spoke.

"You don't need to worry. Just call me anytime, whenever you need to. Okay?" he enquired being concerned.

"Okaay.... Thanks"I said and I hung up the call.

"Pain makes poetry beautiful" This statement of Monica was whirling in my mind since morning. I was in pain. But this pain was not mine. The real person to be in pain was Monica. My pain was just an outcome of concern for her pain and maybe because of this I wasn't able to write anything. I decided to meet her and talk to her.

I went to a renowned painter in a city. I want to gift her a portrait but apparently, I wasn't having any picture of hers.

The painter was asking me too much details. But finally, he painted a portrait of Monica from the clues that I gave him. I won't say that the painting looked exactly like Monica but it was almost like her. It had the glimpse of the mesmerising kindness that she possessed in her soul.

I was finally going to confess my feelings to her and this gift was perfect to come along, I supposed.

I texted Monica to meet me the next day at the side of a lake which was near the mount we trekked last week. She agreed to come.

The thing that was really making me tense was that I couldn't write anything for a long time. I struggled to write but nothing came out of me. I sat near the typewriter for entire night. I scratched my hands with my nails, I banged my head onto the table a hundred times. But nothing came out.

The sun rose and it was time to meet Monica. I went to the same spot. She was standing right there with her back facing towards me. I came out of my car. I looked at her and I realised how much I loved her. I realised there was nothing as painful as her leaving me.

REYANSH's POV

Last week Zubair called me to talk about Monica. He was really worried. But I am happy he finally confessed his feelings to Monica. He called me today and told me that they have decided to move in and that Monica will be living with Zubair forever. I rushed to his house. I wanted to see them together and I wanted to see Zubair happy. Also, this was the first time I was going to see Monica. I have never seen her even in photo since Zubair didn't have any.

I reached to Zubair's place. His car was standing outside. Just when I was passing by the car, I saw the back seat was painted with blood. I was terribly shocked. I started thinking of all the worst possibilities. I rushed to the door.

I knocked it several times. I rang the bell. But there was no reply. I stood silent for a moment. I was able to hear the voice of typewriter and fingers tapping it with a really fast speed. The door wasn't locked. I opened it. I went to Zubair's study. He was sitting right there intensely drawn into writing. He was crying miserably. I saw a girl's body with a knife stuck in her stomach. I was shaken. I felt like nothing was visible to my eyes. I fell on ground.

When I woke up, my head was aching badly. My vision was blur. I managed to pick myself up. Zubair was still there on his typewriter. I asked, "Zubair... Zubair. what happened Zubair? What is all this?" He didn't reply anything. He was crying. His hands were soaked in blood.

There was portrait of a girl on a chair beside. The girl in the portrait was the most shocking thing ever. It was Lisa's portrait. Lisa was Zubair's girlfriend in college. When we were in final year, she died in a car accident. Zubair had been in a long phase of depression after that.

The girl's phone vibrated. It wasn't locked. There were hundreds of calls and messages. I read all the chats in her phone. Zubair's chat was nowhere to be seen. After reading the chat I came to know that the girl came to meet a friend near the lake and she wasn't Monica.

I opened Zubair's Phone.

I opened Monica's chat. I was shocked. In the whole chat, it was Zubair who had been texting. There was no replies. In fact, the messages were never delivered.

I checked call history. Zubair had called on that number a several times. But the calls were never connected.

I checked the number on truecaller. It showed an account with name Lisa Hugo. Lisa was girl who ditched Zubair. He has been imagining her. The girl on the floor was just a victim who came in front of him. It could have been any other girl. The girl was a part of the poetry club too. but the portrait had Lisa's face in it. it was clear that he had been imagining this unknow girl for Lisa.

I checked his phones gallery. There were few pictures of the places where he said he and Monica went for date. In all those pictures, I could see only Zubair.

There was no one else.

I realised all this time Zubair had been hallucinating Monica. But why did he kill that unknown girl?

Suddenly Zubair called my name.

"Reyansh"

"Reyansh, I killed her. You see that knife; I didn't even confess her what I had to say. You see, now I don't have to struggle to write. I have pain inside me. And pain makes poetry beautiful."

"Pain makes poetry beautiful"

This used to be Lisa's opening line in every poetry competition in college days.

I didn't know what to do. I was shock stricken. My head started thumping again with immense pain. I held my head with both the hands. I sat on the sofa in the living room. I was unable to think. Everything went blank.

I checked for pulse and heartbeat in that girl. I called police, doctor and one of her friends. As soon as the doctor came, he confirmed that the girl wasn't dead. They rushed her to hospital and she was admitted in the intensive care unit of the hospital.

Police came and arrested Zubair. He was in custody.

The page on the typewriter read,

"The sins that we think of committing,

But often forget to commit,

These are the lumps that form demons inside us,

The pain that was supposed to be shred,

The pain that came to the tongue but was never freed,

These are the wounds that find no healing,

The times when we tried to rise above,

The times when we showed our wings but we slipped to fall,

These failures have taught me how to unfelt victories,

What passes by rarely fades,

It lives and builds a home inside us,

It resides in our bones happily,

While we linger around to find reasons to be alive.

Mercy?

Where do you fetch mercy from?

Probably from the uncommitted crimes that form demons inside you,

Or from the caged pain that you loved all this while,

Or from the scratches that had forgotten how to heal,

Isn't wrath a kind of mercy in disguise?"

5 years later

The trial is over. They have announced life imprisonment for Zubair. The girl was I come for almost a month but she recovered later. She was present there at time of judgement. She a budding writer now and Zubair a criminal. The poetry club that he owned was sealed and shut.

"Why did you do all this? What's wrong with you Zubair?" this was the first time I went to talk to Zubair after the whole fiasco happened.

Zubair said nothing and he was staring at the ground. I thought he is not going to answer.

"There's a draft in my cupboard that isn't complete. It's a love story I was writing back then. Ask Lisa to complete it. There's a collection of poetry too. The last poem that I wrote, I want all of them to get published in the name of Lisa Hugo. Will you please ask Lisa to do it?" He spoke. Before I could say anything, the police took him into the cell.

"There's no Lisa, Zubair" I whispered as he walked away.

SPRINKLED AND STRIKED: 10 PETALS AWAY

TWO

INTOXICATION OF CERTAINTY WITH MIST

"stop it! Stop it I say!! Help! Somebody please Help!ssssTTOoop!!"

I woke up, finding myself screaming those words. It felt like something was choking my windpipe severely. Although I didn't feel the presence of any physical thing around my neck, I felt something was present. It's really difficult to explain in words. It was kind of a feeling that basically felt like something was trying to smother me, it was there, without being physically present, it was there. The attempt of smothering was a determined one. I felt like I was going to die in another few seconds. I looked around. There was no one around. The environment completely serene and silent. Then what was the thing I felt. Was it yet another nightmare?

Well is wasn't. whenever you are attacked by a nightmare,

your mind wanders out of reality for a few seconds. However, after those few seconds, you can completely feel the present, the physical presence of reality. But what I felt was completely different. Though my eyes were able to perceive the reality, I was able to see that there was no one around, I could see serenity and silence around, but my mind was under strong phase of rejection, absolutely not ready to accept the reality. I felt scared as if something would try to kill me again. I didn't know the reason. I didn't have enough enemies who would try to kill me. But still I was being assassinated or at least an attempt was being made and that too a really determined one. yes, it was intense and determined. I had no clue about anything. The more I thought of what I felt, the more I was surrounded with confusion and the feeling of being near to death hyped.

I looked out of the window; it was still dark. Moreover, I felt like I had slept only for few minutes. I opened my phone to check the time. 3:12 it said. My feeling was right. It had only been half an hour since I went to sleep. To be honest, I didn't even feel like I had been completely asleep. I closed my eyes in an attempt to sleep again. Within another few minutes, I had another and yet more terrible attack of the same feeling. This time with some different visual effects. I saw somebody outside my bedroom, probably a woman. I couldn't recognise her. My brain was not able recollect any of the feature that her body presented to my eyes. She was just terrible. It wasn't that she looked terrible. She was probably there to destroy me and that was something that made her terrible. she tried to come near me. And every step of hers taken towards me was just a booster for my fear. She was scary. There was probably no particular reason behind any of these happenings and this fact scared me the most at that time. I closed the door of my bedroom, I started shouting and screaming for help again. I ran towards the door to the balcony. I tried to open, but couldn't. The door was blocked. It wasn't opening. I started hitting the door with all my energy poured so that somebody could hear me and come for help. A terrible noise surrounded invaded my brain. All my attempts to save myself appeared to be a failure. The door to bedroom broke.

I woke up to find myself alone in bed. It was still dark outside. I again picked up my phone to check the time, 3: 37 it read. I looked around again. Serenity and silence again. I felt irritated to hail. There was no one around and the door to balcony was closed. There was no one outside the bedroom. I close my eyes to recollect what happened to me. I couldn't. All I could see was myself being locked in a room. Somebody had forcefully locked me inside and all I was doing was screaming and crying. Patting the door as hard as I could. Loud noise of door being hit, stroked my ears. The noise kind of numbed my brain. I felt weak, like never before. Seemed like my end was near. I could see it. It was like I had been standing on a cliff. I saw a way back but I couldn't take that path.

Something stopped me every time when I tried to go back, something with hell lot of strength. I had no other choice but to jump off the cliff.

After all this, it was obviously pretty hard to fall asleep again. I tried to sleep but the same view, the same story was constantly running inside my mind.

"I needed to save myself."

THREE

The First Ordeal

"If you're reading this note, I believe most of the things have already been destroyed. Things were over ages ago. But if you're reading this, there's no chance of their slightest existence.

Sprinkler 1:

There was no sun in your garden from very beginning. But still; somehow there were some stubborn rays that always wished you to be in warmth. These rays are no more stubborn. They've faded and you've felt them fading away. Yet you never chose to capture them. I don't blame you dear. I know that these warm rays had at once tried to burn your sweet little forest. I know you were never at fault; nobody ever was. It's just that sometimes life presents you with situations where you can never win, but you don't even loose, where you have to fight constantly, for no reason, as if, as if all you have to do is to try to capture air in your fist. You have to, like a fool child. We all have to. All this is really difficult to say and even more difficult to understand and maybe this is why we're constantly trying to run away from something that doesn't exist. All this delusion, it seems madness. But at the end of the day, we have to realise the fact that all this madness creates a non-existent world in our souls. And once it is created, life becomes really hard because this illusional crypt is going to collide with reality all the time. Reality will try to engulf a piece of it all the time, and every part that merges with reality will leave bruises on your soul. Bruises that are permanent and painful, that never heal. You'll be able to hide them with your happiness sometimes, but they will be stubborn and will keep you in grief for most of the times.

Strike 1:

You don't need to find me. You can't.
27, Tiara street, Ricky gardens
Just write "received 1" on a paper and drop it to above address with a rose petal.

Dated: 11 august 2013"

I found this note in the letter box. Whatever happened last night was extremely terrible. And now I woke up to this. Something strange is happening. Something I want to run away from but I just can't. I hide the note inside the cupboard in my bedroom. It's Sunday today and like every Sunday I'm supposed to spend the whole day with mom, cooking and doing all the crazy stuffs and listening to her cute innocent talks. But today, after the events that took place at night and after receiving such a mysterious letter, I don't think I can live in present completely. Moreover, I

need to check out the address given in the note.
My mom woke up and like every Sunday I made my favourite coffee for both of us. We sat in balcony silently. She was trying to experience the essence of every sip and I was thinking about all the events and wondering the reasons behind all these happenings. I was terribly lost. In another one hour we had our breakfast. It was quite clear from my behaviour that something was wrong with me and my mom already asked me three time if everything was alright.
For one second, I thought of pouring my heart out in front of her. But I couldn't or to be more accurate I didn't wish to. What I was experiencing was quite dangerous and I didn't wish to involve my mom in all this.

I told her that one of my office colleagues was severely ill and so I had to go meet him. This was the simplest reason I could manage to think of to find an escape.

Ricky gardens is almost at a drive of two hours from my house. It's one of the poshest societies of the town. I opened the note once again to confirm the address.

"Dated: 11 August 2013'

I stare the date for almost 5 minutes. The letter was written 6 years ago, the date suggested. But what made the sender to wait for 6 years or was it just another lie. Finally, I reached the destination, the address in the note. To my amusement, 27, tiara street, Ricky gardens was nothing but a large piece of abandoned land amidst tall buildings. Although I should have been surprised, but I wasn't. last 12 hours had already been hell of a ride and I had experienced enough strangeness that this time even the presence of a ghost in front of my eyes was not going to surprise me.

The land was having tall boundary with a metal plate that was blank. It was probably supposed to be a name plate. But it was blank. There was large gate made up of metal rods. It was open. There was no lock. The lashes were open too. It seemed like somebody has intentionally kept it open, for a visitor. I opened the gate and entered that abandoned piece of land. The entire land piece was filled with tall grass. How can somebody drop a small piece of paper there? I looked around to find a safe place to drop a note. I cross checked the address a hundred times to make sure I was at the right address. I kept looking around. In one of the corners, I finally saw a red cross on the boundary. On reaching the spot I saw a small wooden box. It was quite clear that the box was there for the note to be dropped. I opened it and kept the note there. There was no one around. But it was very clear that `everything was well planned. I walked out of there. In my entire journey back to home, I kept wondering about everything that has happened to me over past 20 hours, right from the nightmares to empty metal plate to the red cross and the wooden box. Everything was so hard to believe and digest. Much harder was to accept the fact that all this was really happening to me. I was finally able to feel the reality. Strange right?

All this started with a nightmare that took me away from reality and now I was thrown into the hands of reality mercilessly. What sort of game was this?

I don't have answers. Just questions which have no answers but consequences and these consequences are questions much more difficult to answer.

I reached home. It was quite dark. I realised the day was almost going to be over. Mom was sitting on the sofa, reading some random magazine. I ran up to her and hugged her tightly. I was very close to crying but I didn't. I didn't have enough strength to repeat whatever has happened to me over past one day. I know the solution to all this was not at all easy to find. So, narrating all that would only mean that I was choosing to go through the whole terror again.

"I'm sorry ma. I know this was supposed to be our funky and crazy Sunday. I am sorry I spoiled it." I almost fumbled as I said this. It was clear from my voice that something was wrong.

"you're tired darling. I can sense that from your face and voice. Stop thinking about everything so much. You need to relax. And we had spent enough Sundays together making them as funky and as crazy as we are. So, missing out on one Sunday is not a big deal." She said and her tone was so comforting that it engulfed all the terror and mist in me for few moments. I felt relieved for few moments. I felt like I was almost dead. But her voice filled me with a little life.

"Well the Sunday isn't yet over and so we are going to make dinner together and will play our favourite crazy and funky songs till 12." I said with utmost pretence, putting all energy in pretending to be happy and completely alright.

Both of us burst out laughing.

FOUR
The Second Ordeal

Sleeping for me now was an extreme sport. Not an easy task at all. I was fed up of closing my eyes and seeing a movie that was tearing every inch of my soul apart. I looked at the phone to check time. It was 4:00 AM. I suddenly heard the bell ring. I got up immediately. My heart was beating really fast. The echo could be easily felt. I closed my eyes and asked myself to relax. I wasn't having enough courage to open the door. Leave opening, I didn't even have the courage to walk out of my room. The bell rang again. The fact that there was somebody at my door at 4 in morning was really suspicious and whatever happened in last one and a half day made this fact a terrible one.

Finally, somehow, I built the courage to get up from my bed. I walked towards the door when I heard the bell ringing again. I looked out through the peephole. There was no one outside. Though I saw a shadow near the letter box on the main gate. I closed my eyes to gather courage and finally I opened the door.

No one was there. No shadow anymore. I immediately ran towards the letter box. There was an envelope again, as expected. I opened the envelope. There was a large two-paged letter in it. It would have taken a lot of time to read it. More than reading, understanding has been the real game till now. So, I went back to my bedroom. I switched the lamp on. I could not switch on the light as it would have attracted my mother's attention. I sat on my bed.

"Sprinkler 2:

It was great to know that you've accomplished the first strike successfully. All this is really scary for you and this is going to be even scarier as time passes.

Anyhow, you've to accomplish 10 strikes to get near the end. The game is long and you've to be strong. Otherwise, it's very easy for things to get over. How would you not know this? You've mastered the art of ending things. Isn't it?

You know a garden is just an over nourished, overpampered piece of land. It looks beautiful. This is a fact. It's easy to destroy it, a bigger fact and sometimes the destruction is beautiful. Don't be shocked! You've experienced its beauty. But no matter how beautiful a thing is, it'll have scars. I was that scar in your life.

I had probably been the destruction too. Sometimes it's important to destroy things, everything. Sometimes the trail is very narrow. Walking over it suffocates. You've breathed through all the hard times. I am glad. You're still breathing. It's not everybody's cup of tea. People are fragile, easy to break. It's easier to keep them intact, a fact very few people realise before reaching the end. You're one of god's favourite child, who understood this at a very small age.

Maybe that's why you still have the strength to sit quietly and read this letter. Everything is confusing right? Well you'll figure everything out after the tenth note.

Dated: 12 December 2013."

STRIKE 2:

Reach 27, Tiara Street, Ricky gardens at 10:00 A.M on the coming Sunday. Write "received 2' on a piece of paper with a rose petal.

I folded the note back and kept it inside the envelope. I kept both the envelopes in cupboard. It was already 5:30 A.M. I was supposed to reach office at 8 o'clock. I hadn't slept the whole night and I didn't even wish to sleep now. But I was kind of exhausted. This wasn't the kind of exhaustion where your muscles ache, not the kind where you need rest, not the kind where you can seek help, not the kind where you can hope to get recovered. This was the kind of exhaustion where you want answers, where you're fed up of life, where living is a burden, where dying seems easier.

There were certain things that were clear after reading the letter.

First, the person writing these letters was somebody I knew. He was calling himself a scar in my life and that person has certainly brought destruction to me. my life was going pretty well before this saga started. So, I basically had no idea what that person was talking about.

Second, the person writing these letters, kind of, didn't intend to hurt me. in fact, it felt like he was giving me signs or was trying to tell me something, probably trying to clear some of my doubts.

Well, nothing apart from this was clear. So, all I had now was an extra bunch of questions with uncertain answers. I was thinking about reaching the destination on the coming Sunday because at this time all I wanted was to solve my life.

A week passed. How simple that sentence is, isn't it? Well, the whole process of living it wasn't easy. With turmoil and delusion all around, it felt like I had been suffocating for very long. It was like I was suffering from something incurable where I searched for medicine constantly. I searched for the cure everywhere, right from the first thing that used to come in front of my eyes in mornings to the darkness that I saw and felt after closing my eyes at nights. A week passes, with great difficulty.

The good part was that my mom had to go to my maternal grandma's house as my grandma wasn't well. She said she would be coming back only when grandma will be completely fine. So, I had plenty of time to solve the mystery that I was certainly living.

It was Sunday and I was supposed to reach the spot (21, Tiara Street) at 10 A.M. it was already 7.

I drove to the destination.

The place was same like the last time. The only difference being that this time there was a man standing in front of the gate to abandoned land with a gift in his hand. I walked towards the man.

"Good morning!" he said gently. I looked at him. He was an old man most probably in his 80s. he had slight brown complexion. His face and skin of the hands were only visible part of his body. He was wearing a dark brown coat that descended below his knees. He was wearing black coloured boots. I tried to read his face as carefully as I can because all I wanted now were answers and I was in no mood of gathering an extra bunch of questions.

"A very warm and good morning to you. Seems like you've been waiting for someone." I tried acting as though I went there for the first time. I tried to keep myself calm and acted oblivious.

"No, not really." He said and his left hand slid into a pocket of his coat.

The man seemed in a hurry as if he had very less time left to complete some important tasks.

"Well, you can tell me if you want to find out something" I said comforting him. I intended to help him. But more than that I wanted to know if he had any link with whatever I was going through.

"Well, yes. I've been waiting for someone." Finally, he said hesitantly.

“Who? Who are you waiting for?” I asked him. I was very sure that this time I failed to act normal and the ocean of curiosity spilled out along with my words.

“Oh! I was just passing by here when somebody came and gave me this gift pack. He said that there will be a girl coming here to drop a note with “received 2’ written on it and with a rose petal. I am supposed to give this gift pack to her.” He said as he took out a small box wrapped in glittering sheet usually used to pack gift. There was a note over the gift pack which read

“With love,
From Shaina Martin.”

“I think you’re supposed to hand it over to me” I showed him the rose petal and the note I that I had in my pocket.

The man gave me the gift pack and started moving in his direction. I was completely unaware of what to do next.

“Listen, do you have any idea who that person was, the one who handed this over to you, the gift pack” I said those words in a hurry and more than that nervousness was dripping out of my voice and expressions.

“Well, as I said, I was just passing by child. I wish I could answer your questions, but trust me I don’t have any clue who that person was. Whatever I did was just an act of kindness and courtesy. I felt like helping him. That’s it.” The old man said comforting me.

"You're lying. I know you know me and you know a lot about why I'm here. Just tell me who're you?" my voice was shivering as I said this, my tone was high. It was quite clear that my heart was filled with fear and anger.

'Calm down, child. I am Joseph Brown. I live nearby and I have a small confectionary. If you want to talk about something, you can some along." His voice was so mesmerising. He seemed concerned. It was really difficult for me to not to believe him.

I gathered strength and spoke "Look, we have got not business together. I don't trust you and the fact that you're somehow linked with whatever is happening, this fact makes you the person I shouldn't trust. Not this easily."

"I need to go. This is my address; in case you wish to see me." He snuffed while he handed me card with his name, phone number and address.

I drove back home. It felt like somebody has sucked everything out of my soul, like I was being smothered. There were breaks in breath. I could feel strangulations all over my body. My soul was aching. My brain was failing to respond as if it was just ready to shut down. I was lying on the couch and opening my eyes required too much of energy. Mom was still at grama's house. I didn't eat anything for almost 20 hours. There were two pieces of papers on the table in front of me. One that had "with love, from Shaina Martin" written over it and the other which had the address of the old man. I had no idea what to do with both of them. All I knew was that any moment from now, they could be another letter in the mail box which is going to make things even worse.

FIVE

THE THIRD ORDEAL

The alarm clock was ringing in the bedroom. I had no idea as of when and how did I fell asleep. I checked my phone. There was a miss call from Mom. I called her. We had a normal conversation. She seemed fine and that was a big relief for me. Probably she was the only person who could fill life into my draining soul. There was message too, from an unknown number.

"Reach Stone and feathers garden at 5 P.M." the text read.

I asked one of my friends to find out about the number. I got to know that the number was from a rehab, "Reincarnations". It was the same rehab where my father died. I looked at the message once again. "Stone and feathers garden". It was the same garden where I met my dad for the last time.

He left us when I was 12. From then, I had been living with my mom. I won't say that we weren't happy. We were more than happy together. But what's missing is always missing. We can try hard to find alternatives to fill that gap, the void that has been created. But what's missing will always be missing. The last time I saw him was 5 years back, in 2015, when he died, in the rehab, "Reincarnations". All this while it was really difficult for m and my mom to cope up with everything. There were days where it felt like I couldn't see anything. Sometimes when I look back, I wonder how much I have endured. I never knew I was this strong. I always thought that something drastic might happen and I would just give up. But, after whatever happened, I never gave up. That is something I am proud of. This is probably the reason why I am withstanding all the uncertainties that surround me now. My next target was reaching stone and feathers garden.

I reached the destination on time. A message popped in my phone. "Walk towards the tree in the abandoned are." It read.

I asked the guard about the abandoned area in the garden. The guard said there was a part of garden that got burnt accidently long back. Since then, it has remained like that. I entered the abandoned area. There was a wooden box there too. I rushed towards the box. I opened it. There was a watch and a letter inside the box. The watch wasn't working and was quite old. The letter read,

"I couldn't see you on the day when you were born. I saw you for the first time when you were just 25 days old. You had glaze on your face that was extraordinary. I was scared I might harm you. I had that in my nature. I couldn't help it. I had this illness in me from long back. I never realised, nobody ever realised. By the time we all realised that I need to mended, a lot of things had already gone wrong. I know you aren't brave. But what gives you the strength to stand is that you know how to fight. You take all your injuries and you cry over them. Since you were a little child, I have seen you embracing your wounds, the smallest of them. There have been people in this world, the majesties, the warriors, the inventors. All of them were extraordinary. Some of them were intellectually extraordinary and others were physically extraordinary. I have known you for being emotionally extraordinary and that my dear is a boon.

You might sometimes think, that this world has nor place for things that are soft and fragile. But look around. flowers never resist the forces that tear them away. Nature has a law, "every little thing that happens to be beautiful is soft and fragile." It's all about finding strength in this fragility. The world will fool you. It will teach you to be hard, to be hard on everything. It will teach you how to be hard on yourself, how to be hard on situations and others. But remember, softness is an epitome of love and everything that loses love is no less than a corpse. Be soft.

18 January, 2014."

The letter was written on my birthday. I next thing that I had on my mind was going to the "Reincarnations" rehab. It was very clear now that whatever was happening now was linked to my father. The letters, they seemed like somebody was writing them on his behalf.

When I reached rehab, the first thing I did was to enquire about the number from which I was receiving texts. After a lot of hustles, the receptionist told me that the number belonged to one of the psychiatrists who worked there but now had left the job. On asking about the name, he told me that the number belonged to Dr. Shaina Martin. It felt like there was no ground under my feet, like I was standing on clouds, like I could fall any moment now. I breathed and asked him to give me her address. He did the same. I rushed to Dr. Shaina Martin's place. The lady was sleeping. I waited for her in lobby.

After a period of almost one and half hours, she appeared in front of me.

"Good evening, this is Dr. Shaina Martin. I am sorry I am not practicing these days. But since you're here and it seems like you're in trouble, I would like to ask how may help you?" She asked in a polite tone. It seemed like she had no idea who I was. But I would somebody send texts to a random person?

"I have been receiving some texts from a number and I doubt it happens to be yours." I said in a firm voice. When I showed her the number and the texts that I had received, she just turned away. It was clear from her expression that she had been doing all this stuff. The next shocking thing that happened was Joseph Brown coming down the stairs.

"I knew you had something to do with all these miseries in my life. What game have you both been playing and what do you want?" I shouted. I was scared as hell. There were a lot of facts in front of me now. But none of them had answers to the questions that were there inside me.

"Sherlin (name of the protagonist), why do you think your

father left you?" She asked while she looked into my eyes.

"It had got nothing to do with you." I tried to be as reluctant as I can be.

"Look if you don't answer my questions, your questions will remain unanswered too. There's a reason why all this is happening to you." She said in a tone of affirmation.

"He wanted to live his own life. He wasn't happy with us. That's all I know. That's what he said when he left us. That's what my mom has told me in all these years." I answered.

"Sherlin, I was person who was treating you father. He came to rehab when he left both of you. He had this psychiatric illness which made him impulsive and indecisive. I had seen him for 4 long years. In those seven years all he intended was to be better, a better person for you. The letters that you had been reading were the letters that he wrote in the course of his treatment. He left you and your mom because his illness was making him abusive. He tried staying away from both of you. He was tired of making you people suffer because of his illness. Your mom tried to find him quite a lot of times after he left. But she could never reach us. Joseph was your father's best friend. I tried to reach up to you and your mom but you father always refused. The only person I could reach was Joseph, who had seen and visited him in 4 years of his treatment. It was two years before his death when he was diagnosed with cancer and that's when he realised that he had no more time to be a better person. He knew he had very less time left. He wanted to meet you but at the same time he knew that after all the bad memories that you had with him; he knew you wouldn't show up. But he wanted to make you aware of his love and his experiences of life, something that a child needs to learn from a father and so he wrote these ten letters. The two rose petals that you dropped with the previous two notes were for his grave. The last thing that he wanted was to see you. He wanted you to read all those ten letters and he wanted you to keep ten rose petals on his grave, one after you receive each letter. He said that this was something that was going to make his soul aware of the fact that he had taught you something.

He wanted to be a good father for you, when he was alive and even after he died." She spoke.

She gave me rest of the ten letters. I read all of them only to find out that his abusive behaviour was nothing but an outcome of his illness and that he loved me, mom and all his friend too much. I didn't come to his funeral because I always blamed him for making my mom miserable. I remembered the times when she used to cry to sleep on a daily basis. I visited to cemetery; I visited his grave for the first time. My mind was crowded with a lot of memories. I sat there and embraced his grave. It felt like I was hugging him for the first time. I cried my heart out and everything went blank.

9 798886 679335

Printed by Libri Plureos GmbH in Hamburg, Germany